PETER POWERS™

and the Swashbuckling Sky Pirates!

PETER POWERS™

and the Swashbuckling Sky Pirates!

**By Kent Clark
& Brandon T. Snider
Art by Dave Bardin**

Little, Brown and Company
New York Boston

Copyright © 2017 by Hachette Book Group, Inc.
PETER POWERS is a trademark of Hachette Book Group.
Cover and interior art by Dave Bardin
Cover design by Christina Quintero
Cover copyright © 2017 by Hachette Book Group

Little, Brown and Company
Hachette Book Group
1290 Avenue of the Americas, New York, NY 10104
Visit us at LBYR.com

First Edition: December 2017

Little, Brown and Company is a division of Hachette Book Group, Inc.
The Little, Brown name and logo are trademarks of Hachette Book Group, Inc.

Library of Congress Cataloging-in-Publication Data
Names: Clark, Kent, author. | Snider, Brandon T., author. | Bardin, Dave (Illustrator), artist.
Title: Peter Powers and the swashbuckling sky pirates! / by Kent Clark & Brandon T. Snider ; art by Dave Bardin.
Description: First edition. | New York : Little, Brown and Company, 2017. | Series: Peter Powers ; 6 | Summary: "When a group of sky pirates steal everyone's abilities, Peter must help his family, save his friends, and battle the diabolical Sky Pirates without using his powers." —Provided by publisher.
Identifiers: LCCN 2017005956| ISBN 9780316437943 (hardcover) | ISBN 9780316437936 (trade paperback) | ISBN 9780316437912 (ebook) | ISBN 9780316437929 (library edition ebook)
Subjects: | CYAC: Superheroes—Fiction. | Ability—Fiction. | Family life—Fiction. | Pirates—Fiction. | Humorous stories. | BISAC: JUVENILE FICTION / Action & Adventure / General. | JUVENILE FICTION / Humorous Stories. | JUVENILE FICTION / Readers / Chapter Books.
Classification: LCC PZ7.1.C594 Pes 2017 | DDC [Fic]—dc23
LC record available at https://lccn.loc.gov/2017005956

ISBNs: 978-0-316-43794-3 (hardcover), 978-0-316-43793-6 (pbk.), 978-0-316-43791-2 (ebook)

Printed in the United States of America

LSC-C

Hardcover: 10 9 8 7 6 5 4 3 2 1
Paperback: 10 9 8 7 6 5 4 3 2 1

Contents

CHAPTER ONE
Powers Practice

"I CAN'T DO THIS!" I moaned.

I'd been running around the backyard all afternoon. I was trying to steal a flag from Dad's hand. Despite many attempts, I hadn't snatched it yet. My parents were teaching me some brand-new hero skills. That way, I wouldn't have to rely on my ice powers all the time. But the only thing I'd learned so far was that I'm *not* so great at Capture the Flag.

Who am I? I'm Peter Powers. I've got ice

powers and they're *awesome*. Slowly but surely, my parents have been training me to use my abilities for good. Mom and Dad are big-time heroes, so they know what they're doing. Actually, my whole family has powers. We're super—with a dash of weird.

"You can do this. Take a deep breath," said Mom. "Remember how I taught you? In through your nose and out through your mouth."

"Why can't I try out my famous moves like the Blizzard Blast or the Storm of Icicles?" I pleaded.

"You don't *have* any famous moves, Peter," Dad reminded me.

"*Yet*," I countered.

"Charge at me again—and *no ice powers*," Dad said.

"But they're my *thing!*" I shouted in frustration. "They're all I've got!"

"Take it easy on yourself, son," he said. "Stay focused and remember: You can do anything you put your mind to. You're Colonel Cold, the Icy Avenger!"

I love Dad's sense of humor. He always knows how to light a fire under me, and not just because his power is to create flames. As the superhero known as Fireman, he protects Boulder City from all kinds of danger.

"Lame name, Dad!" my older brother,

Gavin, groaned. He burst from the back door in a hurry.

"Yeah! Lame name, Dad!" another Gavin said, following the first one. Soon a fleet of Gavins poured out of the house like mice. My older brother has the power to clone himself. He likes to use his duplicates for mischief.

"Where do you think you're going?"

Mom inquired.

"Football game," Gavin answered. "It's the Gavins versus the Gavins."

"No clones in public, Gavin. You
know that. We've got secret identities to
protect," Mom said.

"Ugh. Fine!" Gavin said, stomping on the
ground to make his clones disappear. He ran
off in a huff while I got back to my training.

"Have you chosen a superhero name yet,

Peter?" Mom questioned.
"It's always good to be
prepared when the time
comes. Any ideas?"

"Of course I have
ideas. I have *all* the
ideas," I said. "But nothing
feels right so far."

"A newscaster gave

me the name Flygirl when I first started out. It wasn't my favorite," Mom explained. "That's why I've given myself a brand-new name. Now I'm officially AERO-WOMAN."

I liked Mom's new name a lot more than the old one. She did too. It made her feel powerful.

CRASH!

A commotion came from inside the house. "Sorry!" shouted my sister, Felicia. "I accidentally threw the fridge across the kitchen, but I'm putting it back!" Felicia's power is super strength. She doesn't know how to use her abilities very well.

"Clean up your mess, Felicia, and get

started on your chores," Mom scolded.

Felicia stomped through the house, shaking the whole thing. "Enough with the stomping. You'll wake Grandpa and your baby brother from their naps."

My baby brother, Ben, has the power to turn invisible. It makes him quite the handful. Grandpa Dale lives with us and takes care of us whenever Mom and Dad do their hero thing. He's a retired super-hero and the coolest grandpa ever.

"Chores sound fun. Can I do those instead?" I asked.

"No," answered Dad. "No more distractions. And no superpowers."

"But my powers are awesome!" I pleaded.

Dad moved into position. "LET'S GO!"

I closed my eyes, held my breath, and charged toward Dad. As he ducked to avoid me, I tripped over his foot and fell flat on my face. It was *really* embarrassing.

"I call that move the ol' Duck and Trip," Dad joked. He tried to make me laugh, but I wasn't in the mood. Dad offered me a helping hand. "You okay, buddy?"

"No," I said. "My powers are what make me special. Without them, I'm just another dumb kid. I don't understand why I have to keep doing this."

"Because you are *more* than an ice maker, Peter," said Dad. "By the time your training is over, we'll have unlocked so many new skills, you won't know what to do. I know it's difficult, but you've got to be patient with yourself. You can do this!"

Dad wanted to bring out the best in me. And he was right. I couldn't give up so easily.

"Why don't Gavin and Felicia have to train?" I asked.

"Because they don't want to be heroes. You *do*," Mom answered. "That's why Dad and I want to help you become the best hero you can be."

"Less chatting and more charging!" Dad said with a grin. He held up the flag. "Come and get it."

I dusted myself off, took a deep breath, and charged my dad once more.

CHAPTER TWO
The New Kid

At lunch the following day, I couldn't stop thinking about my failed training session with Dad.

"Peter. You're not eating your Yummy Bun," Sandro whined. "It's a beautiful pastry filled with gooey cream. If you don't put it in your mouth within the next minute, I'll consider it a crime."

Sandro is one of my two best friends in the entire world. He's also one of the hungriest people I've ever known. He'd eat a brick if it had frosting on it.

"It's all yours," I said. "I'm not that hungry." Sandro snatched the tasty treat and put it on his lunch tray.

"What's going on, Peter?" Chloe asked. She's my other best friend and a computer whiz too. There isn't much that Chloe *can't* do. She's the smartest kid in school.

"Nothing," I said, staring out the cafeteria window.

Chloe didn't believe me. "Not eating dessert?" she asked. "You're definitely stressed out about something. I'm guessing your *no powers* training session was a bust."

"What's the point of having super-powers if I can't USE THEM?!" I asked. "They're all I've got. What am I without them? I'll tell you—a *big nothing*."

"Don't say that!" Chloe didn't like it when I talked down about myself. "You're funny, smart, kind—"

"Don't forget *weird*," interrupted Sandro.

13

"You're so much more than your super abilities, Peter," Chloe said, giving me a pat on the back. "You're special with or without them."

"Superpowers are supercool," Sandro said, letting out a smelly burp. "End of story."

"*You* don't have powers, Sandro. Does that make you *uncool?*" asked Chloe.

"Probably," Sandro said, taking a gulp of chocolate milk.

"Sandro, you're funny. Chloe, you're smart. But I'm *nothing* without super-powers," I said, slouching in my seat.

"Excuse me," a voice said. It was the new kid in school. "I'm Ed Chang. Were you talking about superpowers? I'm a *big* fan of superheroes. I can barely fit my comic book collection in my new closet."

"Mind your business, new kid," Sandro said. "I'm trying to eat."

"It's nice to meet you, Ed," Chloe said, extending her hand for a shake. "Don't listen to Sandro. He's in the middle of a sugar rush. It affects his brain."

"His superhero name could be the Cake Devourer!" Ed giggled.

"Hey, Peter. Maybe Ed can come up with a superhero name for you," Sandro said in between bites. Chloe kicked Sandro under the table. "Ow! Why'd you kick me?!"

Chloe and I stared at Sandro. Only Chloe and Sandro knew about my secret superpowers. Ed certainly didn't.

"What Sandro means is, I *wish* I were a superhero," I said.

"Me too!" Ed said. "Hey, is that a Yummy Bun?"

"Hands off!" Sandro yelped, nabbing it off his tray and swallowing it whole.

Ed laughed. "I wasn't going to take it. My grandma makes them from scratch. I've got a million at home."

Sandro's eyes began to sparkle. "A million Yummy Buns? Sit down, Ed! Join us. Perhaps tomorrow you can bring one for each of us."

CHAPTER THREE
Uncle Stuart

DING-DONG!

My siblings and I looked at each other. We weren't expecting anybody. Gavin cloned himself, sending his dupe to answer the door. "Uncle Stu is in the house!" Gavin #2 shouted.

We all jumped up and ran to see our favorite uncle. Dad's brother, Uncle Stuart, is an adventuring daredevil. He's explored worlds beyond imagination, and his stories are some of the most epic

18

tales ever told.
Not only is Uncle
Stu a world-class
fighter, he also
has a cool sword
collection.

The Lost City of Lionex is beautiful this time of year!
—Uncle Stu

"Ick!" Felicia winced. "Uncle Stu, you're covered in goop."

"Oh, that? HAH!" Uncle Stu guffawed. "That's just a little ectoplasm. I got stuck battling a fleet of Ghost Elves on the way over."

"You're late," Grandpa barked, rolling through the house in his wheelchair. "Hurry up and get to the dinner table, swashbuckler. I'm starving!"

"You look well, old-timer," Uncle Stu said, smiling.

"I've got your old-timer right here, you long-haired braggart!" Grandpa wheeled over Uncle Stu's big toe. Grandpa and Uncle Stu love to joke with each other. "I was saving the world when you were in diapers."

"What did you bring us?!" Felicia asked, rudely reaching into Uncle Stu's knapsack.

"Felicia!" Mom yelped. "You don't reach into someone's private belongings like that. Go wash up. Stu, you should wash up too. I hope you brought your appetite."

Uncle Stu rubbed his belly. "You bet I did!" He chuckled.

Uncle Stu told so many amazing stories over dinner, I could barely keep up. First, he told us how he tamed the Cat People of the Lost City of Lionex. Then he described the night he battled a band of mutant marauders. And he had a sword duel with

an evil genie to save a princess. Finally, he told us a story about spending time among the peaceful Wind Specters of Cloud Mountain. It made me want to be a superhero so bad. I wish I lived a life as exciting as Uncle Stu's. He's kind of my idol.

"YAWN," Grandpa said in an exaggerated tone.

"Uncle Stu, will you take me on an adventure sometime?" Gavin asked.

"What Uncle Stu really needs is someone strong like me," Felicia said, flexing for Uncle Stu.

"Felicia, Gavin, you two have homework," Mom said. "Get to it."

Luckily, I'd already done my schoolwork. Now I could spend extra time with Uncle Stu. "How do you do it?" I asked. "You don't have superpowers."

"Who cares?!" Uncle Stu said, cocking his head at me. "Who says you need powers to be a hero?"

"Oh...well...um," I stammered.

"Listen up, Peter. A real hero has *skills*. No powers needed," said Uncle Stu. "You've got to keep your mind sharp and be quick on your feet. Heroes aren't born—they're made."

"You're an inspiration," I said. "I wish you could stay forever. So what brings you to town? Another adventure, I bet!"

"Didn't your dad tell you?" Uncle Stu said, giving me a hearty slap on the back. "I'm here to train you, Peter. We start bright and early tomorrow morning. You're going to love it."

CHAPTER FOUR
Names and Games

"Get up, lazybones. Today is the first day of the new you," said Uncle Stu. I was still in bed when he'd barged into my room. He took one look at me and shook his head in disbelief.

"Let's go. Up, up, up!" Uncle Stu picked up my sketchbook and flipped through it. It was filled with costume sketches and superhero names. I usually kept it hidden so my siblings wouldn't make fun of me.

"That's nothing," I said. "Just some ideas I'm working on."

Uncle Stu furrowed his brow as he read my to-do list: "'#1: Create an Igloo of Solitude. #2: Battle a galactic warlord for control of the galaxy. #3: Freeze Gavin solid.' HAH! Those are some big goals!"

Uncle Stu flipped through to my list of possible code names. "'SNOWY FROST-MAN: ICE MASTER SUPREME'?" he read, pretending to be afraid. "Sounds *scary*."

To Do List
#1: Create an Igloo of Solitude
#2: Battle a galactic warlord for control of the galaxy.
#3: Freeze Gavin solid.
Possible Code Names
Snowy Frost-Man: Ice Master Supreme
S.F.M.I.M.S.

"I'll take that, thank you," I said, grabbing the notebook from Uncle Stu's hands.

"What's wrong with Peter Powers?" Uncle Stu asked, taking a seat at the end of my bed.

"I'm worried about my future as a superhero," I answered.

"No, I meant what's wrong with using *Peter Powers* as your superhero code name?" asked Uncle Stu. "It's solid. It's a name that says, 'Get out of my way, I'm saving the day!'"

"*Peter Powers* is boring," I moaned. "I want a name with flavor! I need it to be bold and fresh!" I hopped out of bed and did a dramatic superhero pose.

"Salad dressing has flavor that's bold and fresh. How about *you* be yourself?

That's a good place to start," Uncle Stu said. "Now, put some pants on and meet me outside in five. We've got work to do."

There was no turning back now. I got dressed, then went outside. Uncle Stu had created an obstacle course in the backyard. It had a rope ladder, a tunnel tube, and even a giant wall. It was awesome—until I realized that I was the guy who had to complete it. The more

nervous I get, the more I sweat. Before I knew it, I was totally drenched.

"I can't do this," I said, turning to head back into the house.

"Relax, Peter," Uncle Stu said. "Give it a shot. Trust me on this. I've got your back."

Even though training was a big pain in my rump, I knew Uncle Stu wouldn't steer me wrong. He believed in me, even if I didn't

believe in myself. I shook off my worries and got my head in the game. "Let's do this," I said, getting into starting position.

"Attaboy!" Uncle Stu cheered. "Show me who you are without your superpowers. On your mark, get set, GO!"

I took off like a bolt. But before I got to the first obstacle, I tripped over my untied shoelaces. I crashed right into a mud puddle.

"I'm done," I said, scooping the mud out of my eyes. "I can't do it."

Uncle Stu said, "If you want to be a fierce warrior like me, you're going to have to complete this course. Now get on your feet and try again."

I tried to get up, but the more I struggled, the more I sank. "Don't you get it?!" I finally shouted. "I'm not special without my powers!"

"Being special isn't about having powers," Uncle Stu said. "It's about *using what you have*. Peter, you've got all kinds of skills. They're trapped inside you, waiting to get out. It takes *work* to unlock them, so *work* is what you're going to do. Now GET UP."

He was right. If I wanted to see real change, I would have to work at it. I peeled myself out of that crusty mud puddle and got back into starting position.

"That's the spirit!" cheered Uncle Stu.

"Once this part is over, I'll teach you how to *duel*—with *swords*."

Uncle Stu pulled a small knife from his back pocket. He pressed a button on its handle, and the knife transformed into a huge sword, fit for any warrior.

"I've got a second one," Uncle Stu said, smirking. "It's yours—IF you complete this course."

Finish line, here I come!

CHAPTER FIVE
Pirates in the Sky!

After hours of obstacle coursing and sword dueling, I stank. I was coming downstairs from my shower when I noticed how quiet it was. I asked, "Did everybody go to dinner without me again?"

"Peter, in here, quick!" Gavin whispered. The family was intently focused on the TV.

"We bring you this breaking story from downtown Boulder City," the news reporter began. "Enormous pirate ships have flown out of the clouds and docked themselves above the Museum of Natural History."

"Sky Pirates," Uncle Stu groaned. "I've dealt with these thugs before. They're rude, crude, and stink to high heaven. One time, I—"

"Not now, Stu," Dad said. "Save story time for *after* we've sent them packing."

"PI-WUTS!" baby Ben giggled, pointing at the TV with glee.

Pirates slid down ropes from their flying ships onto the

museum's roof. The rowdy pirates then began breaking into the museum's skylight, just above a display of valuable diamonds.

"That's our cue to suit up and head out," Mom said, turning to Grandpa Dale. "Dad, would you mind keeping an eye on things while we're gone?"

"Yeah, yeah, yeah. At least you asked this time," Grandpa said in a huff. "Next time I'm going to start charging for my services."

"All right!" shouted Uncle Stu. "It's Sky Pirate butt-kicking time!"

"Hey, Dad," I said, tapping him on the shoulder. "Can I come? I promise to stay on the sidelines."

Dad knelt down. "You saw those pirates. This is dangerous business, Peter. Keep an eye on things here, okay?"

In the blink of an eye, Mom, Dad, and Uncle Stu suited up, then flew out of the house. (Well, Uncle Stu didn't fly. Mom gave him a lift.) The rest of us gathered around the TV. It was hard knowing that our parents were out there risking their lives to keep Boulder City safe. It was even harder having to stay at home and watch it on TV. I wanted to be a part of the action.

"Move it!" Felicia said to Gavin's clones. "The couch is for the *whole* family to use, not just your dumb dupes."

"Beat it, tiny! We were here first!"
replied Gavin, Gavin #2, and Gavin #3.

There may have been more Gavins,
but Felicia was stronger than all of them
combined. She shoved them to the floor.
Gavin cloned himself over and over, but
even with eight Gavins, they couldn't
move Felicia. They all started shouting at
her, when I lost my temper.

"QUIET!!!" I roared at the top of my lungs.

"KWAI-UT?" Ben asked, tugging on
the leg of my jeans. I picked him up and
hugged him.

"Not you, little rascal," I said.

"MAMA ON TV!" Ben cooed, pointing
at it.

Mom, Dad, and Uncle Stu were facing off against the Sky Pirates. Dad blasted the invading hordes with his fire powers. Mom flew forward, bowling over the villains. Uncle Stu laughed as he dodged pirate swords left and right, protecting the museum staff. Dad guarded the diamonds while Mom swooped in and out of the horde of attacking pirates to throw

them off balance. My superheroic family seemed to have everything under control. Still, I was worried.

"They're the best in the business, kid," Grandpa said, patting my back. "Heroes through and through! Even that blowhard Stu. They'll beat those stinky pirates and come home safe and sound."

The pirates were making their escape. Dad used his fire powers to fly after them. He was almost at their closest ship when—*SHAZACK!*

A bright red laser shot from the pirate ship. It blasted Dad in a burst of crimson light. Suddenly, he was falling out of the sky.

Mom swooped in and caught him. But when he tried to use his powers again, nothing happened.

"Is he okay?!" Felicia asked.

"No," I said, horrified. "He's *powerless*."

CHAPTER SIX
Dad Down

"Clear the couch!" Uncle Stu roared.
He kicked open the front door and was
carrying Dad in his arms. "Wounded Dad
coming through!"

"Is Dad dying?!" Felicia cried.

"DAD IS NOT DYING!" barked Mom.
"He got hit with a beam of energy that
stole his powers. That's all."

"That's all?!" I said.

Uncle Stu carefully laid Dad onto the

couch. He was groggy but alive. "Did we win?" he asked, rubbing his head.

"They didn't snatch the diamonds," Uncle Stu said. "Not on *our* watch."

"Who are these Sky Pirates?" I asked. "I've never heard of them before."

"They're a bunch of rude, nasty ol' thieves. It's all steal, steal, steal with

them," Uncle Stu explained. "They've got no respect for the law or anything else. If someone has something they want, they'll find a way to snatch it—by any means necessary."

Mom looked shaky. "But how did they steal my husband's powers?"

Grandpa quietly wheeled himself over. "The Mystic Rune of Zaldor!" he said. "I'd know that red beam anywhere. *That's* what stole his powers."

"The Mystic Rune of Zaldor? That means big trouble," said Uncle Stu. "Its origin is a mystery, but I know that it can drain all sorts of energies. I guess that includes superpowers."

"We have to get Dad's powers back," I said. "What do we do?"

"*You* aren't doing anything," said Mom. "Uncle Stu and I will figure out a way to get Dad's powers back. *You're* still training."

"This is the perfect chance for me to use my powers. You need the extra muscle," I said.

Mom let out a big, long sigh. "Peter, we go through this every time. You're not ready to be a full-fledged superhero yet. I appreciate your passion, but the answer is no." Then she turned her attention to Gavin and Felicia. "You two aren't taking after Peter, are you?"

"*Ew*, no!" Felicia gagged.

"No way, we're not the ones who want to be heroes," Gavin reminded Mom. He exchanged a strange look with Felicia. They were up to something, but I didn't have time to investigate. Not with Dad's powers on the line.

"The Sky Pirates have been around a good long time," Grandpa said. "Almost as long as me. I bet if they came to town to steal some diamonds from the museum, they won't give up so easily. They'll be back."

"Then let's be ready," Mom said. "Dad, if you think of anything else, let us know. In the meantime, Stu, make some calls. Call every hero, villain, and weirdo you know. See if you can find out anything else. In the meantime, I'll take care of my husband," Mom said.

"What can the rest of us do?" I asked.

"Peter, just keep being you. Make sure your brother and sister act normal at school tomorrow. Okay?" Mom said, putting her hand on my shoulder. "And PLEASE promise me you're not up to something."

"I'm not up to anything," I said. "I'll stay out of trouble."

"I have your word?" Mom asked.

"Yes, I promise," I said. Lucky for her, I was a man of my word.

CHAPTER SEVEN
The Family Secret

The next day at school, Chloe and I met at our lockers. She had seen the news, but I filled her in on everything else.

"What if Dad never gets his powers back? He'll have to get a job. Or worse— he'll lay around all day like a lump. I'll have to spoon-feed him his meals like I do with my baby brother," I said. "This is a nightmare!"

"Get a grip, Peter," Chloe said. "None of that is going to happen. Your dad is

going to get his powers back, okay? I
want to hear you say it."

"My dad is going to get his powers
back," I repeated.

"Feel better?" Chloe asked.

"Not yet," I said honestly. There was so
much on my mind that I thought my head
would explode.

"I can't imagine how Dad must feel
right now. My powers are lame, but I'd
be destroyed if I lost them. Dad must feel
totally lost."

Chloe put her arm around my shoulder.
"I'm going to be really honest, Peter," she
said. "Superpowers aren't everything.
It's *awesome* to have them, don't get me

wrong, but they're only *part* of who your dad is as a person."

"Why does everyone keep saying stuff like that?" I asked.

"Because it's true," Chloe said. "Look at me. I don't have powers, and I'm totally awesome."

That makes sense, I thought. Dad had super awesome fire powers, but he never stopped learning new skills. He always strove to be better—not just as a hero, but as a person. I was beginning to see why he wanted me to study and train so badly.

"You guys!" Sandro said, sneaking up behind us. "I've got the *biggest* news! I'm starting a brand-new diet!" Sandro did a happy dance.

"No way," Chloe said. "Really?"

"Yes way!" Sandro said. "It's called the *seafood* diet…"

Chloe rolled her eyes. We'd both heard Sandro tell this joke a hundred times. "Don't say it," she warned.

"…because whenever I SEE food, I EAT it!" Sandro cracked up.

"You are such a cornball," Chloe said, shaking her head.

Sandro sniffed the air around him. "Mmmm. Cornballs," he said. I quickly told him about Dad. He snapped out of his food trance and got serious. "How's your dad feeling, Peter? Must feel odd to have superpowers one minute and *nada* the next."

"Talking about superpowers again?" Ed Chang called out. He had a habit of popping up at the wrong time.

"Hi, Ed," Chloe said. "What's up?"

"Did you see the big battle on TV? Fireman was totally *POW! ZAP! KAPOW!* with those Sky Pirates yesterday! But rumor has it he's totally powerless and giving up the superhero business," Ed said. "At least, that's what I read on the Internet."

"Don't believe everything on the Internet," I shouted, louder than I meant to. "Fireman is NOT, I repeat, NOT down for the count."

Ed gave two big thumbs up. "Awesome," he said. "I'm happy to hear that."

"Peter, chill. Your dad will totally get his powers back. I can feel it in my bones," Sandro said.

"*Dad?*" asked Ed. His eyebrow rose with suspicion.

I panicked. Luckily, Chloe jumped in

for the save. "What Sandro means is that Peter's dad had an accident," she said, trying to craft a realistic cover-up. "He hurt himself pretty bad. Since he can't go to work, it's like he's without his 'powers.' Get it?"

"Um, sure," Ed said.

"Who said anything about Fireman? I said, he's on FIRE, MAN!" Sandro said, trying to help. But it was only making things more uncomfortable. I reached into his backpack, pulled out a Yummy Bun, and stuffed it into his mouth.

RIIIIIIIIIING!!!

The school bell meant it was time to split up. Chloe grabbed her books from her locker, then left. Sandro skipped away, happily munching on his Yummy Bun. Ed and I stood together in awkward silence. He seemed like a nice kid, but I couldn't tell him about my family. "Well, I've got to go," I said.

"Me too," Ed said. "I hope your dad feels better."

Yeah, I thought. *Me too.*

CHAPTER EIGHT
Life Lessons

"Okay, now parry!" Uncle Stu shouted.

"Who's Perry?" I asked.

"No, *parry*, with an *a*. It means to ward off an attack," my uncle explained. He used his own saber to show me the move. "Do it like this."

It had been almost a week since the Sky Pirates skipped town. But they left a dark cloud hanging over Boulder City. My family was waiting for them to return to try and finish the job. We were also waiting for a chance to get Dad's powers back. In the meantime, Uncle Stu had been using his free time to train me.

After I (finally) aced the obstacle course, he'd agreed to teach me to duel with swords. Just with wooden sabers—no transforming swords yet. Swordplay was

hard work, even when practicing. I was exhausted and out of breath. "I need to sit down for a minute," I said.

"C'mon, Peter," Uncle Stu said. "Do you think the bad guys are going to take it easy on you?"

"Probably not," I said. "Luckily, you're not a bad guy. Thirty seconds' rest, okay?"

"Fine, you sit there and I'll practice what we'll be doing next." Uncle Stu ran, leaped into the air, pushed off the side of our house, did a front flip off a tree branch, bounced off another branch, did a spin-kick off the telephone pole, and then landed on the roof.

Then he did a backflip off the roof and landed on the ground. "Ta-da!" he said with a dramatic bow.

"You want ME to do THAT?" I asked. "No way."

Uncle Stu laughed. "I thought the same thing the first time I saw it. It's called parkour, and it takes practice. Lots of practice. But get good at it, and maybe you can use it to save the world one day."

"Me? Save the world? Yeah, right," I

said. I'd always dreamed of it, but the closer I got, the further away it seemed.

"You will, Peter. One day," said Dad. I was so in my head that I hadn't noticed Dad watching us from the back door. "Do you remember that video game Frankenstein Shark Attack? As you'll recall, I couldn't figure out that combo move to save my life. You had to teach it to me over and over again. Remember?"

"Of course I remember," I said. "That was my favorite game. We used to get up early and play a few rounds every day before school. It took you *forever* to get that move right. But once you did, you kicked butt all the way through level five."

"Exactly," Dad said. "And how did I manage to get that move right?"

"Practice," I said. "And lots of it." I finally saw his point. I had to keep trying.

"No more jibber-jabber. We've got work to do," Uncle Stu said. "Anyone who's not training to be a lean, mean hero machine, go inside."

Dad was about to head back in when he stopped. "You know what, I think I'll stay."

"Oh yeah?" Uncle Stu said, tossing a wooden saber to my dad. "Think you can handle this?"

"Easily," Dad said.

Uncle Stu laughed, aiming his saber. "Please. When we were growing up, you could never beat me in a sword fight."

"That's because you cheated." Dad smirked, raising his sword.

"Well, if you think you can beat me now, you should try," Uncle Stu said, smirking back. They shook hands, then moved into fighting positions.

"And...GO!" I said.

Uncle Stu's and Dad's swords hit each other over and over and over. They struck and parried all over the yard, back and forth. Uncle Stu was obviously the better swordsman, but Dad was trying his hardest. It looked like Uncle Stu was going to win—but at the last second, Dad ducked and swept his foot across the ground, tripping Uncle Stu. Uncle Stu hit the dirt.

"Not bad, brother," Dad said, helping him up.

Uncle Stu laughed. "You've gotten better in your old age."

"Who you calling *old*?" Dad laughed. Then he turned to me and said, "See, who needs superpowers?"

CHAPTER NINE
A Plan Hatches

Training with Uncle Stu was fun—but exhausting. My feet hurt. My legs hurt. My arms hurt. Actually, everything hurt. Yeesh.

With so many moves to remember, I started practicing before bed. I tried doing it outside, but Felicia and Gavin would watch me through the windows and make fun of me. So tonight, I decided to do it in my room. I grabbed my wooden practice saber and did the meditations my uncle showed me.

Take a deep breath, I thought. *In through your nose and out through your mouth.*

"*KI-YAH!*" I said, kicking into the air. My leg hit the glass of water I keep by my nightstand. It crashed to the floor, shattering to pieces and soaking my rug. "Good job, klutz-bomb," I mumbled to myself. I tiptoed around the glass, then snuck out of my room to find a towel.

Instead, I found my siblings leaning over the top of the staircase. They were up to something.

"What do you think you're doing?" I asked.

"Be quiet, Peter!" Felicia hushed me.

"Everyone is in the kitchen," Gavin said, "talking about the Sky Pirates."

"So? What do you care?" I asked.

"Mom said YOU couldn't help out. She didn't say anything to us," Felicia noted.

"Since when do you want to be heroes?" I asked. "That's *my* jam!"

"We can't let you have all the fun," Felicia said.

"Plus, if we said we wanted to be heroes, Mom and Dad would make us train. No thanks," Gavin said.

"You two are the worst!" I said, more annoyed with them than usual.

Felicia clapped her super strong hand over my mouth. "*Shhhhhh*," she hissed.

Downstairs, the adults were talking. "...we've got to *rush* these Sky Pirates, get the Mystic Rune of Zaldor, and destroy it," Uncle Stu said. "It reminds me of the time I wrestled Avianne the Bird Lady. Her wingspan was forty feet. There were feathers everywhere—"

"If I hear one more of Stu's stories, my brain is going to burst," Grandpa complained. "Rushing in isn't a plan. You are out of your mind."

"You're just jealous because I'm so handsome," Uncle Stu said.

"Hah!" Grandpa laughed. "You'd be jealous if you knew who I was dating... Lady Diablo!"

"No way!" Uncle Stu said. "She turned me down!"

"Let's stay on track, gentlemen," Mom said. "We don't have time for silly squabbles. Uncle Stu's informant found out that the Sky Pirates are returning. Tomorrow at three PM, they'll attack the museum at the exact time the guards plan to move the diamonds somewhere else. We need to be there to make sure the Sky Pirates fail."

"What's the plan?" Dad asked.

Mom always had a plan. She was awesome like that. "Dad wants to come out of retirement for this one. (Guess we'll need a sitter for Ben.) At the museum, Dad will be in the air on the north side. I'll be in the air on the south side. You and Stu will be on the lawn, for ground support."

"Let's do this!" Dad said.

Gavin whispered to me and Felicia, "What a dumb plan! Uncle Stu and Dad don't have powers—they'll get creamed."

"They'll need help," Felicia muttered.

"No way," I said. "They've got this.

Powers or no powers, Dad is a superhero."

"Yeah, right," Gavin said. "Without powers, Dad couldn't even take me on."

"Is that so?" Dad asked, standing at the bottom of the stairs and looking up at us. "I may not have my fire powers, but I can still hear three kids who should be in bed."

"What are the three of you doing?" Mom asked, joining Dad.

Felicia fell silent (for once). Gavin said, "Uhhhh...sleepwalking!" Then he ran back to his room. No surprises there. Our parents turned on me, expecting an answer.

"We're inspecting the walls for, uh...
termites," I said.

"Sure," Dad said, rolling his eyes. "Stop
snooping and go to bed. All of you. We'll
be up shortly to say good night."

Felicia and I trudged back to our rooms.

"Termites?" groaned Felicia. "That's all
you could come up with?"

"At least I said something!" I argued.
"But seriously, you and Gavin *cannot* get
involved tomorrow. It's dangerous. Promise
me you'll stay out of it." I hoped Mom's line
to me would work on my sister.

"Whatever," Felicia said, then
slammed her door in my face.

Guess not.

CHAPTER TEN
The Decision

"DRAMA!!" said Sandro.

"There's no drama," I said.

"Not yet," Sandro said. "But you just told me and Chloe about your family's plan to stop the Sky Pirates. And how your brother and sister are totally going to crash the fight. So, no, no drama yet—but there will be!"

"You don't think Gavin and Felicia are dumb enough to show up, do you?" I asked.

Chloe and Sandro looked at each other,

then both nodded. "Your brother once drank a bottle of ketchup because you told him it was a magic potion," Chloe said.

"Good point," I said. "This isn't good. They could get seriously hurt. But I can't try to help. My mom made me promise. What should I do?"

"What do you *want* to do?" Chloe asked.

"I want to help. Duh!" I said, throwing my hands up in the air.

"Look, Peter. You've come a long way with your powers. But do you really think you could go up against a band of marauding Sky Pirates?" Chloe asked. "Your parents told you NOT to get involved for a reason."

"Another good point," I said.

"What does *marauding* mean?" asked Sandro.

"It means they're dangerous," Chloe answered.

"Then HECK YES you should help!" Sandro cheered. "Going up against dangerous bad guys when the odds are stacked against you is what superheroes are supposed to do!"

"You have a good point too," I said to Sandro.

"Peter isn't a *superhero* yet, remember? He doesn't even have a code name," Chloe said.

"I'm working on that," I said.

"*And* you don't have a costume," Chloe reminded me.

"I have my hoodie and mask! And I've got *heart*. That counts for something!" I proclaimed.

"Your heart is leaking," Sandro said. I glanced down but nothing was there. "HA! Made you look."

"Peter, if you fell for that, you're definitely not ready for Sky Pirates. You're still in training. If you make the wrong move, people might get hurt. You don't want to carry that burden."

It came as no surprise that Chloe was right again. "So Sandro votes yes, and Chloe votes no. And I'm still on the fence.

I wish someone could break the tie," I said.

"My vote is YES!" said Ed Chang, popping out from behind a locker.

"What'd you hear?!" I asked. If Ed kept appearing like this, he was going to find out about my superpowers.

"Nothing really," Ed said. "But saying yes is always more exciting than saying no. But that's just my opinion." Ed reached deep into his backpack. "By the way, I brought these Yummy Buns for you."

Sandro's eyes got so big, I thought they would pop out of his head. *"Gimme, gimme!!"* he shouted. Grabbing all three of the tasty treats, he shoved the Yummy Buns into his mouth at once. "More? Do you have more?" Sandro asked, still chewing.

"Oh. No. I only brought three, one for each of you," Ed noted.

Chloe and I glared at Sandro. "Well, thanks anyway," I said to Ed.

"Any time. I hope you figure things out, Peter," he said. "The world can always use more heroes." Ed gave two thumbs up and ran off to class.

"I'm really starting to like that guy!" Sandro said, his face covered in Yummy Bun.

"Peter, what are you going to do?" Chloe asked.

I didn't have an answer. What Ed said, about the world needing more heroes—I agreed. And Dad said I was a hero with or without powers. I didn't want to break my promise to my mom. So maybe if I stopped Gavin and Felicia *before* they went to the museum—then I could save the day without breaking my promise. That's what I would do. What could go wrong?

CHAPTER ELEVEN
Assault from Above

After school, I chased Gavin and Felicia. "Hey, wait up," I said breathlessly. "Last night, you two made it sound like you were going to the museum to fight the Sky Pirates. Were you serious?"

"No way. The museum is for learning," Gavin said.

"We'll leave the superhero stuff to the professionals," Felicia added.

"I'm so relieved," I said. "It would be

dumb to rush into danger, especially without training."

"You're right, Peter," Felicia said. "As always."

"See ya at home," Gavin said.

Gavin and Felicia got their bikes and waved good-bye. I sat on the curb and waited for Sandro and Chloe. The three of us always rode our bikes home together.

"Hey," Chloe said. "Did you talk some sense into your brother and sister?"

"I did," I said, impressed with myself. "They're finally listening to me. And they were so nice too."

Chloe gave me a strange look. That's when I realized... "Wait a minute," I said. "Since when did my siblings start listening to me? And they're never nice to me...."

Sandro pointed. "And they're not riding toward home. They're riding toward downtown. Isn't that where the museum is?"

"They lied to me!" I said.

"What time is it?" asked Chloe.

"Almost three o'clock," Sandro answered.

"They're going to try and stop the Sky Pirates," I said. My throat started to close, and I could feel a pit growing in my stomach. I tried hard not to panic.

"Peter, you're sweating like crazy," Chloe noticed.

"And ice cubes are popping out of your fingertips," Sandro added.

"I have to stop them!" I said. I hopped on my bike. I pedaled as fast as I could, but time was running out. Overhead, the clouds darkened, and pirate ships flew out of the sky. I pedaled harder and harder, as hard as I'd ever pedaled in my life. A few minutes later, I arrived at the Museum of Natural History. But the battle had already begun!

One of the Sky Pirates' ships dropped an enormous anchor down onto the roof of the museum. Hundreds of ropes launched from the ship, and a battalion of pirates descended to the roof and the ground.

I saw Mom and Grandpa swoop in to

stop them. Meanwhile, Dad and Uncle Stu were battling pirates on the front steps. They were back-to-back, swords out, dueling with the raiders.

That's when I saw Gavin and Felicia rush in to help.

Felicia knocked out four pirates with one

punch. Gavin multiplied and turned into an army of ten, all of them fighting the pirates. I would have been proud of my family if I wasn't so scared. As I ran to help, something in the sky caught my eye—a red glow from the central Sky Pirate ship. It started to grow. I recognized that red light. It was the same

color as the blast that depowered Dad. "Oh no," I whispered. "The Mystic Rune of Zaldor is getting ready to fire!"

I ran across the museum lawn toward my family. "Get back, everyone! They're about to—"

SHAZACK! SHAZACK!

The bright crimson laser zapped Gavin and Felicia first. They fell to the ground in

a weakened state. Felicia could barely lift her head, and Gavin's dupes had vanished. Despite the danger, I ran to check on them. "Are you okay?" I asked.

Felicia slowly opened her eyes. "I feel really tired," she moaned.

"My powers are gone," Gavin said.

Suddenly, Mom and Grandpa swooped down from the sky. Dad ran toward us on

foot. I was happy to see my parents, but I didn't have time to explain the situation.

"What are you doing here?!" Mom yelled. "We told you kids not to get involved!"

"We didn't listen," Felicia said. "Peter tried to stop us, but we didn't listen—"

SHAZACK! SHAZACK! SHAZACK!

More blasts from the Mystic Rune of Zaldor. Mom and Grandpa got zapped. And so did I.

I felt instantly cold. I tried to use my powers, but I couldn't even make a single ice cube. I was powerless.

And now a gang of Sky Pirates was headed our way, fast. Even in her weakened state, Mom had a plan.

"Peter, listen closely," she said. "Find Uncle Stu. He'll know what to do. Dad and I will protect your brother and sister."

"But who will protect you?" I asked.

"Go NOW!" Mom shouted. I ran toward the steps, where I'd last seen Uncle Stu. As I turned back, I saw my family surrounded by Sky Pirates.

They tossed a net on them and lifted Mom, Dad, Grandpa, Gavin, and Felicia up into the air. The look in Mom's eyes told me she had a plan. I didn't know what it was, but I knew I couldn't hold back any longer.

The *city* needed me. My *family* needed me. *No more Mister N-Ice Guy!*

CHAPTER TWELVE
POWERLESS!

The Sky Pirates were invading the entire area. As I looked for Uncle Stu, a Sky Pirate spotted me. "You're coming with me, matey," he growled.

"KI-YAH!!!" roared Uncle Stu, swinging onto the scene. He kicked the snarling pirate right in the face, knocking him to the ground. Another took his place, and soon Uncle Stu was fighting hordes of pirates. He jumped and flipped over them with ease. One pirate jabbed his fist in Uncle

Stu's direction, but my heroic uncle caught
the punch and gave him a butt to the head.

"Uncle Stu!" I cried.

"Peter?" Uncle Stu said. "What are you
doing here?"

Before I could answer, two pirates
grabbed Uncle Stu's arms while two more

held his legs. I looked up to the sky and saw the red glow again. Uncle Stu broke free of the pirates' grasps and tossed his enemies into a pile. "Uncle Stu, watch out!" I shouted. I ran toward him and tackled him, knocking him out of the way of the blast.

"Thanks for the save, kiddo," Uncle Stu said. "But not necessary. I don't have any powers. That gemstone's got nothing to take from me."

Suddenly he looked at me differently. "You're a hero, kid! You know what you need to do now. Fire up those ice powers and give those Sky Pirates a cold shower." Uncle Stu chuckled.

"Um, I kind of got blasted already," I admitted. "I'm powerless."

"No, you're not," he said. "Remember your training. And remember fast. We've got company." Then he tossed me his extra transforming sword.

More pirates surrounded us.

"FREEZE!" I shouted. But when I aimed, nothing happened. In the heat of battle, I sort of forgot I had lost my powers five minutes ago.

All the Sky Pirates started laughing. One of them laughed so hard he cried.

"Poor little kid thinks he's a superhero!" one pirate cackled.

"Take another step, and I'll destroy you,"

I yelled at the top of my lungs. "I may not have powers, but I can still take you!"

"Nice gusto," Uncle Stu said. Then the pirates attacked. Uncle Stu did most of the work. But I helped. Kind of. Mostly by staying out of the way. But I did battle one pirate with an eyepatch. He wasn't a very good sword fighter—but neither was I. We parried and struck with our sabers.

Eventually, he poked himself in his only working eye and tripped, knocking himself out.

"Behind you, Peter!" Chloe shouted.

A giant pirate swung his sword, and I ducked just in time. Then I hit him where it hurts—right between the legs. The giant pirate fell to the ground, moaning in pain.

"Nice one!" Sandro said.

"What are you doing here?!" I yelled.

"We followed you in case you needed help."

"Um, so did I," Ed Chang said, popping up behind them.

"All of you have to get out of here! It's dangerous!" I shouted.

"What he said," Uncle Stu agreed. He was busy fighting the last of our attackers.

Suddenly, three more burly pirates showed up and grabbed Sandro, Chloe, and Ed from behind. They tossed my friends into a net. "More hostages!" the head pirate shouted to the ship immediately above.

"Peter, help!" Chloe screamed.

As I ran toward them, the net was pulled into the sky. I watched helplessly as my friends were taken to the same ship as the rest of my family.

CHAPTER THIRTEEN
One Last Shot

Uncle Stu and I finished fighting a crew of pirates. When we looked up, another group of Sky Pirates walked out of the museum with diamonds. They climbed onto their ropes and were pulled up into their giant ships in the sky.

"They have the goods," Uncle Stu said.

"Who cares about the diamonds! They have our family! They have my friends!" I shouted. "What are we going to do?"

CLANKITY CLANK! CLANKITY CLANK!

CLANKITY CLANK! The Sky Pirates were retracting their giant anchor from the roof of the museum.

"They're about to leave!" I shouted. "We have to get up there! But how?"

Uncle Stu gazed up at the main flying pirate ship and got very serious. His eyes darted in every direction, looking for...

"There!" shouted Uncle Stu. "It's old but it'll do the job." He pointed at the giant catapult in the museum courtyard.

"Are you insane?" I asked.

"You bet I am," Uncle Stu said, running to the catapult. "Come on!"

I ran after Uncle Stu, my stomach in knots. "I don't know if I can do this."

"Peter, once those pirates take off, there's no telling where they'll go. They'll demand ransom for your family and friends. That catapult is the quickest way up!"

I looked up. The pirate ship's anchor was almost totally retracted. We had no powers. Everyone else was captured. We had to save them. "Okay, let's do this," I said.

Uncle Stu made sure the catapult was aimed in the right direction. Then he and

 I hopped on.

"It's now or never!" Uncle Stu said. He used his sword to cut the

rope. The catapult flung us into the air!
Twenty feet. Fifty feet. A hundred feet! I
tried not to look down.

"Yahooooooo!" Uncle Stu screamed
with joy.

"Yahooooooo!" I started to scream too.

We grabbed on to the enormous anchor.
Uncle Stu and I clung to it as it was pulled
up into the Sky Pirates' ship. As soon as
we were inside, we were surrounded by
an army of angry pirates.

"I'll handle these freebooters," Uncle
Stu said, whipping out his transforming
sword. "You find that magic rock. I bet
it'll be stashed in the captain's quarters.
When you have it, smash it!"

"Smash it?" I asked. "But we need to get everyone's powers back!"

"Trust me on this!" Uncle Stu said. "Now GO!" He pushed me into an empty hallway and slammed the door shut. The sound of fighting started on the other side of the door. It was all up to me....

CHAPTER FOURTEEN
Face-Off

The inside of the Sky Pirates' ship was a
scary place. As I hurried down the darkened
corridor, furry little critters scurried across
my toes. The smell was bad too. I tried not
to inhale. I had a mission to complete, after
all. At the end of the corridor, I noticed a
large wooden door. It said CAPTAIN'S QUARTERS
on it. *Well, that was easy*, I thought. I pushed
the door open and walked inside.

Nobody was there. Was I really this lucky?
I scanned the room. The chamber was

filled with loot, stolen from our planet and beyond. Golden goblets, glowing gems, and ancient weapons lay in piles surrounding a golden throne. But just as I spotted the Mystic Rune of Zaldor, on a table in the far corner, I heard a flush!

The bathroom door opened. A stinky smell came out, followed by a giant Sky Pirate. He was almost seven feet tall and had a huge beard and a peg leg. "Hello, lad. Welcome to the lair of Captain Peg-Leg Plunder,

the most fearsome Sky Pirate in all of history!" the gruff pirate huffed, plopping down onto his throne. "And who might you be? One of my new cooks?"

"I don't work for you. I'm one of the good guys. My name is Peter Powers," I snarled in a threatening tone. "You have my family and my friends. I want them back."

The captain began laughing. "You're but a flea. What makes you think you can demand anything of me? I know you got zapped by my Rune of Zaldor. You're powerless. But I like your attitude. I tell you what—pay their ransom, and you can all go free. Otherwise, you can join them."

I needed to smash that rune. But it was on the table behind the pirate. Normally, I would use my ice powers to freeze the bad guy in place or snow-blast his eyes. But he was right—I was powerless. Well, I was without powers, but I could still be me.

As part of my training, Uncle Stu and Dad had both told me to always keep a villain talking. They said it would keep them distracted. So that's just what I would do....

"Wait a minute. Did you just come out of the bathroom? You didn't wash your hands, did you? That is *soooo* gross."

"I'm a pirate. We're a filthy people. We never wash our hands!"

"Nasty," I said. "But nice place you've got here. How did you get this stuff?"

"I'm an amazing pirate, you dummy! The best in the biz! Take a gander at my loot. Who do you think stole all these piles of jewels? This guy!" Plunder said, pointing to himself.

"Do you enjoy your job?" I asked. "I've been thinking about a career change, myself. Maybe I should be a pirate. Looks like it pays well."

The Sky Pirate captain seemed to tear up. "Don't look at me!" he growled, turning away. "I'm not crying, it's just my allergies."

Plunder was acting strangely, but I

wasn't going to let it distract me from my mission. I had to get my hands on the rune. As I edged closer to the table and the rune, I kept him talking.

"You sure? You seem upset."

"Pirating isn't as fun as it looks. It's work, work, work. But I don't have any other skills. Never thought I needed 'em," admitted Plunder. "I never learned to paint. I never learned to play the clarinet. I never even learned to fight! I have my crewmen fight for me. Sad, right?"

While Plunder's back was turned, I carefully tiptoed over to the Mystic Rune and slipped my hand under the glowing red stone.

Plunder turned around in an instant. "That's not yours!" he barked.

"Where's my family?" I asked in a threatening tone.

"They're downstairs in the brig, silly," Plunder explained. "Don't worry. There's a TV in their jail cell, and I left them a bag of potato chips. They're fine. You, on the other hand, have a BIG problem."

"Stay back!" I snapped. I tightened my grip on the rune. "I know what this is, and I'm not afraid to use it."

The captain glared. "You don't know how to use it."

"I'll figure it out!" I said.

"That thing isn't mystical, you foolish

boy. It's not a rune! And there's no such place as Zaldor. That thing is just a plain old crystal with a tiny lightbulb inside," Plunder said. "Totally worthless."

But I watched his eyes, which looked the way Gavin's did when he lied: no eye contact. "You're lying," I said.

Plunder lunged toward me and reached for his property. Before he could grab the rune, I ducked out of the way, stuck my leg out, and tripped Plunder with my foot—just like Dad showed me. The pirate captain crashed to the floor. His peg leg flew off his knee and landed at my foot. I thought, *Why not?*

I lifted the peg leg into the air and then

brought it down, smashing the Mystic
Rune of Zaldor.

A big red flash of light filled the room.
Energy began shooting out of it in all
directions, emitting both steam and
magic. A big white light slammed into me.
I felt energized. But while I was dazed,
Plunder slipped his peg leg back on and
made a run for it. I chased after him,
until we were both on deck. I held up my
hand and said,
"FREEZE!"

My ice
powers shot his
legs, freezing
him in place.

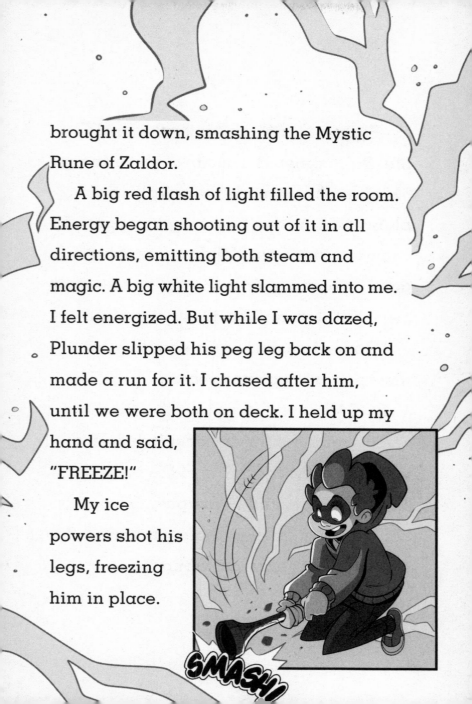

"Right on time, my boy!" said Uncle Stu. He'd cornered a group of shivering Sky Pirates and made them walk the plank. They weren't wearing any pants. I wasn't going to ask. "Did you smash the gem?" he said.

"I did!" I said. "The energy flew out."

"Good, then our family should have their powers back any second."

BOOM!

The center of the deck exploded. Mom and Dad came flying out of the brig. Gavin, Felicia, and Grandpa came out behind them. Then so did my friends— except something was wrong....

CHAPTER FIFTEEN
Reunited

WHOOSH!

Sandro ran past me faster than a speeding bullet. It happened so quickly that I almost lost my balance. "What. The heck. Is going on?!" I asked.

"I can run fast!" Sandro declared. "REALLY fast!"

KRAK-A-DOOM!

The sound of lightning crashed through the sky. Electricity crackled in the

air around us. It was coming from Chloe's fingertips.

"Um, I think I can control lightning," Chloe said.

I couldn't believe what I was seeing. My two best friends had superpowers just like me. A million questions ran through my brain, but none of them made it out of my mouth. "Wha? Huh? Buh?" I stammered. "How?!"

"Peter, when you smashed the Mystic Rune of Zaldor, it released all the stolen superpowers that were trapped inside," Mom explained. "I guess there were some extras in there. That's how your friends got their abilities."

"How many kinds of superpowers were in that thing?" I asked. "Where did they all go?"

"We don't know yet," Dad said. "But I'm sure we'll find out soon enough."

There was one person missing. "Where's Ed?" I asked. After today's adventure, the new kid knew *everything* there was to know about me and my family.

"Down here!" a tiny voice called out

from below. The sound was coming from near my feet. A teeny-tiny Ed hopped into my hand! He was giddy with excitement.

VEROOSH!

In a swirl of energy, Ed grew to normal size. "I can shrink!" he said, giggling. "This is going to be so awesome. I'm finally a full-fledged superhero!"

Mom shook her head. "No, Ed. You're not. None of you are. Listen up, everyone.

This includes you, Felicia and Gavin. Having superpowers isn't a game. It's a big responsibility. If you want to be a hero, then you need to be trained. But first, we'll have to talk to your parents."

An idea swiftly formed in my head. "I'll help train you!" I said with pride. "I mean, I did just save the day *without* powers."

"See? *That's* what makes you special, Peter," Chloe explained. "You want to *help*. No matter what. That's your *thing*, and you don't need powers to do it. Helping people takes patience and courage. That's what makes you a hero in *my* book."

"WARNING! MUSH ALERT!" Sandro groaned.

Uncle Stu gave me a hearty slap on the back. "You faced down Peg-Leg Plunder, kid! What a thrill!" he said. Then he added, "Where did that salty sky dog run off to, anyway?"

We turned around. The Sky Pirate had vanished.

A wide grin formed on Uncle Stu's face. "Perfect." He chuckled. "I'll be the guy who finds him and brings him to justice. I know all the best places to look. He can't hide from *me*."

"Peter, how in the world did you defeat a real-life pirate captain?" asked Ed. "That's super crazy amazing."

"I used an old trick I learned from Dad.

It's called the Duck and Trip," I said. I'd never seen Dad smile so big.

"Big deal. Can we go home now?" complained Felicia.

"I'm so hungry that my stomach is going to eat itself," whined Gavin.

Dad leaned down to whisper in my ear. "I'm proud of you, son," he said. It was the best thing I'd heard all day.

There was one more order of business before we ended our adventure.

"Did you decide on your code name yet, Peter?" Mom asked.

Everyone stared at me. They were waiting for the big reveal. I wasn't about to keep them waiting any longer.

"Actually, I've decided I'm not in a rush for a code name. For now, I'm going to stick with *Peter Powers*. What do you think?"

"Attaboy!" cheered Uncle Stu. "You can't go wrong with a classic."

Everyone chuckled.

"By the way," Mom said to me, Gavin, and Felicia, "you three are soooo grounded."

Meet PETER POWERS!

A boy whose superpowers are
a little different from the rest...
JUN -- 2018